The Tale of
Freddie Firefly

Arthur Scott Bailey

Contents

THE TALE OF FREDDIE FIREFLY

BY

Arthur Scott Bailey

I
A MERRY DANCER

Nobody in Pleasant Valley ever paid any attention to Freddie Firefly in the daytime. But on warm, and especially on dark summer nights he always appeared at his best. Then he went gaily flitting through the meadows. And sometimes he even danced right in Farmer Green's dooryard, together with a hundred or two of his nearest relations.

No one could help noticing those sprightly revelers, flashing their greenish-white lights through the gloom. And many of the field people, as well as the folk that lived in the farmhouse, thought that the dancers made a pretty sight.

But there were others who said that the Firefly family might better be spending their time in some more serious way.

Benjamin Bat, who lived in Cedar Swamp, was one of those who found fault with the merry dancers. He grumbled a good deal about them--and especially about Freddie Firefly.

"He's so proud of that light he carries!" Benjamin often exclaimed, "Now, if he could hang by his feet from the limb of a tree--and SLEEP at the same time--he'd have something to boast of!"

No doubt Benjamin Bat was jealous. Anyhow, Solomon Owl declared that there was still another reason why Benjamin did not like Freddie Firefly. Solomon claimed that Benjamin would have liked to EAT Freddie. But he didn't quite dare to grab him for fear of getting burned by Freddie's light.

If that was so, then it was no wonder that Freddie kept flashing his light in the dark. And it was lucky that he had a light, because--like Benjamin Bat himself--he was a night-prowler.

Unlike Farmer Green, Freddie believed that the night air was very healthful.

And together with all his family, he thought that a damp place was much to be preferred to a dry one.

He often remarked that the pollen upon which he frequently dined tasted best when the dew was upon it. And he never could understand why Buster Bumblebee's sisters, the ill-tempered workers, always gathered nectar for their honey-making in the daytime.

"Everyone to his own taste!" Freddie sometimes said. "And I suppose that those who sleep from sunset to dawn don't know what they're missing."

Johnnie Green, who went to bed almost as early as the Bumblebee family, couldn't help envying Freddie Firefly and all his sprightly company. Johnnie thought it must be great fun to frolic the whole night long--if only Solomon Owl wouldn't scare a person half out of his wits with that unearthly hooting of which Solomon was so fond.

But you may be sure that Freddie Firefly never bothered HIS head over Solomon Owl. Perhaps he knew that Solomon was too busy hunting for mice to take notice of anybody so small as he was, even if he did carry a bright light everywhere he went.

II
A FINE PLAN

Chirpy Cricket was one of Freddie Firefly's neighbors. He was a good neighbor for anybody to have, too, because he was one of the most cheerful of all the field and forest-folk that lived in Pleasant Valley. Freddie Firefly liked him. And he often remarked that he would rather hear Chirpy Cricket sing than sing himself.

Since he was so fond of hearing Chirpy's songs, it was lucky for Freddie that his sprightly neighbor usually chose to sing at night, when Freddie could better enjoy his shrill ditty. And Freddie frequently went out of his way on a fine, dark, summer's night to find Chirpy Cricket and thank him for his kindness.

At such times Chirpy Cricket always smiled mysteriously, saying "I'm glad my voice pleases you." But it must be confessed that he was not singing for Freddie Firefly's benefit at all. He was singing for his own entertainment--and maybe to please some lady of his acquaintance as well. And he chose night time for his chirping because he didn't dare sing during the day. He knew that after sunset almost all the birds were asleep--except for Solomon Owl and Willie Whip-poor-will and a few other feathered folk who preferred the dark to the daylight. They were not so numerous that they worried Chirpy very much. But between dawn and sunset there were altogether too many birds awake to please him. Then Chirpy Cricket kept quite silent. He didn't wish to draw attention to himself by singing, because he didn't care to be gobbled up by any bird, no matter how handsome or hungry the bird might be.

Perhaps it is a wonder that Chirpy could be so cheerful as he was, living under such difficulties as he did. But on the other hand, maybe he felt so carefree at night that he couldn't help being jolly.

Anyhow, he was always ready for a good time. And if there was no good time at hand, usually Chirpy Cricket could think of some sort of frolic.

And so, at last, he hit upon the idea of a torchlight procession. Somebody had told him that Farmer Green's family had seen such a parade in the village one evening. And Chirpy Cricket saw no reason why he and his friends should not enjoy one too, right there in the shadow of Blue Mountain.

"What they can do in the village, we can do here!" he exclaimed. And though it was still broad daylight--being not later than the middle of the afternoon--Chirpy set out at once to find Freddie Firefly, because he simply had to get Freddie to help him.

He found Freddie in the swampy part of the meadow, near the place where the cat-tails grew. And though Freddie was a bit sleepy, he became wide awake the moment he heard Chirpy Cricket's voice.

"I've thought of a fine plan!" Chirpy Cricket cried. "I'm going to have a torchlight procession and I want you and all your family to take part in it."

III
FREDDIE AGREES TO HELP

Never in all his life had Freddie Firefly heard of a torchlight procession-- nor of any other sort of procession, either. So when Chirpy Cricket first mentioned his plan it was no wonder that Freddie looked somewhat blank.

But when Chirpy explained that a procession was a parade, which meant that you followed a leader--and a good many others--in a long line, Freddie Firefly began to understand.

"I need you and a few hundred of your nearest relations to furnish the lights," Chirpy Cricket continued. "And I wish you'd ask your whole family to take part in the procession, for we really can't have too many of you."

"When will the procession take place?" Freddie Firefly wanted to know.

"To-night, as soon as it's dark enough!" Chirpy told him.

"And where are we going to march?"

"Oh, all around the meadow!" said Chirpy Cricket. "The line will form along the stone wall by the roadside. ... Do you think you'll be there?" he inquired somewhat anxiously.

"You certainly can count on me," Freddie Firefly promised. "Of course, I can't very well accept your invitation for more than about fifty-five of my brothers--and maybe six dozen of my cousins. But I HOPE there'll be more of us than that."

"Well, I hope so, too," Chirpy Cricket said. "But even if there were no more than you can promise, we ought to have enough. Fifty-five and six dozen make one hundred and twenty-seven; and you make one hundred and twenty-eight."

"Yes," replied Freddie Firefly, though he thought it would have been more polite had Chirpy Cricket counted him first instead of last, since he was the first of his family to be invited. But he really couldn't be angry with anyone so cheerful as Chirpy Cricket.

"I'll have to leave you now," Chirpy announced, "for I must be on my way. I shall have to make a great many calls before sunset, because I want to invite all my friends to join the procession. ... I'll see you later," he said, as he turned away.

He had not gone far before he stopped and called to Freddie Firefly.

"Don't forget to bring your light with you to-night!" he cautioned him.

"I'll try not to!" Freddie shouted. But if the truth was known, he couldn't have forgotten his light, even if he had wanted to! It was just as much a part of him as his eyes or his six legs. But Chirpy Cricket didn't seem to know that. And Freddie Firefly didn't choose to enlighten him.

Then Chirpy Cricket hurried away. He went straight to the clover field, because he wanted to ask Buster Bumblebee to take part in the torchlight procession. And Chirpy knew that the clover field was the best place to look for him, on account of Buster's being so fond of clover juice.

Reaching the field where the red clover grew, Chirpy began to hunt for the biggest blossom of them all. And when he found it, there was Buster Bumblebee, sitting on top of it and enjoying a hearty meal.

He listened, between sucks at the sweet juice, to Chirpy Cricket's invitation. He seemed interested, too.

"What music are you going to have at your parade?" he inquired, for Buster was very fond of music.

Chirpy Cricket replied that he hadn't thought much about that, but he said he expected to sing.

Buster Bumblebee grunted when he heard that. To tell the truth, he didn't care much for Chirpy's voice, which he considered altogether too shrill.

"Are you going to take part in the procession?" Chirpy asked him.

"I'll let you know to-morrow," said Buster Bumblebee. "Ah, but that will be too late!" Chirpy cried. "We're going to have the procession to- night."

"To-night!" Buster exclaimed. "Then I can't come. For I shall be sound asleep right after sunset."

IV
GETTING READY

Buster Bumblemee's mind was made up. Although Chirpy Cricket told him it would be a shame for him to miss the torchlight procession, which was sure to be a great success, because Freddie Firefly had promised to be there with one hundred and twenty-seven of his relations, Buster still shook his head.

"I wouldn't think of such a thing as staying out after dark!" he declared with much firmness.

"But you ought to see the Firefly family when they're all lighted up!" Chirpy Cricket cried.

"Are they as bright as the sun?" Buster asked.

"N-no--but they're brighter than some of the stars," Chirpy replied.

"Well, I don't care if they are," said Buster. "I need my rest at night. And you'll have to get along without me, though of course, I'm much obliged for the invitation."

Seeing that further urging was useless, Chirpy Cricket left Buster and hurried away to find Jennie Junebug. And to his delight, she said at once that she would be much pleased to attend the torchlight procession. She did wish, however, that he had invited her earlier, because she would have liked a new gown for the occasion.

"Oh, come just as you are!" said Chirpy Cricket.

"What! With my apron on?" Jennie Junebug exclaimed.

Chirpy Cricket went off laughing. Buster Bumblebee had caused him some disappointment. But now he was feeling quite cheerful again.

As he went from place to place inviting his friends to come to the torchlight procession that night, he found that a good many felt as Buster Bumblebee did. They declined to break their life-long rule of going early to bed. But there were others, such as Mr. Moses Mosquito, Kiddie Katydid, and Mehitable Moth, who said at once that they were glad he asked them and that they wouldn't miss the fun for anything.

Meanwhile Freddie Firefly was just as busy as Chirpy Cricket. And he had somewhat better luck. For not only did fifty-five of his brothers and six dozen of his cousins promise to take part in the procession--and bring their lights, too--but at least three hundred others, including some of Freddie's second and third cousins, agreed gladly to join in the evening's sport.

So before dark Freddie sent a message to Chirpy Cricket by Greenie Grasshopper, telling him that he might count on a big turnout of the Firefly family.

That was good news. And Chirpy Cricket felt so happy that he began to sing earlier in the evening than was his custom.

While it was still dusk he went to the stone wall where the procession was to form. And of course he had to wait there a long time before the first of the Firefly family appeared.

Even for a person as cheerful as Chirpy Cricket, it was hard to wait. But he consoled himself by chirping his loudest.

"I suppose Freddie Firefly and all his relations are very busy getting their lights ready," he thought.

At last, when it was quite dark, Freddie Firefly lighted on a head of timothy grass close beside the stone wall and began to flash his light right in Chirpy Cricket's face.

"Here I am, just as I promised!" he called.

V

AT THE STONE WALL

Where's the rest of your crowd?" Chirpy Cricket asked Freddie Firefly, when they met by the stone wall. "It's getting darker every minute. And the torchlight procession ought to start right away."

"They're coming," said Freddie. "If you look sharp you can see them now, crossing the meadow."

Chirpy Cricket tried to see through the blackness of the night. After gazing steadily for a few moments he was able to make out a patch of twinkling lights, which looked a good deal like stars, except that they were too low. Since they kept growing brighter, Chirpy Cricket knew that they must be moving towards him, and that many of the Firefly family had accepted his invitation.

Soon a great host of Freddie's relations surrounded Chirpy Cricket. They flashed their lights in his eyes, so that he was almost blinded by the glare. And it was only with much difficulty that he could see Moses Mosquito, Kiddie Katydid, and Mehitable Moth, who had also arrived by that time.

"What are we going to do?" everybody asked Chirpy Cricket at the same time. So there was nothing he could do but mount the wall and make a speech.

"Friends--" he said, in his loudest voice--"I'm glad to see so many of you present. Our torchlight procession is going to be an even greater success than the one that Farmer Green went to see in the village--if you'll only follow my directions."

"We will!" his listeners cried.

"Please don't ask us to march after dawn breaks, for we'll be ready for bed by that time," Freddie Firefly interrupted.

"I understand," Chirpy Cricket replied. "And now this is what I want you all to do: you must fall in line one behind another. And when everybody's ready I'll take my place at the head of the procession and lead you all around the farm, and right past Farmer Green's window, too."

"Forming a line is going to be hard work," somebody objected.

But Chirpy Cricket arranged that matter simply enough.

"Just form your line along the stone wall" he directed them. "The wall is straight enough. And to tell the truth, that's exactly why I told Freddie that we'd meet here."

"But what about Moses Mosquito and Kiddie Katydid and Mehitable Moth?" Freddie inquired somewhat anxiously.

"Well, what about them?" Chirpy asked him. "What do you mean?"

"They haven't brought any lights," Freddie pointed out. "So what's the use of their being in the procession?"

"Oh, that's all right!" Chirpy Cricket assured him. "They're going to carry the banners."

VI
THE BANNERS

When Chirpy Cricket mentioned "banners," Mehitable Moth, Kiddie Katydid, and Moses Mosquito stepped forward with looks of pride on their faces-- so far as one could see their faces by the glimmer of the flashing lights of the Firefly family. And at the same time Freddie Firefly shouldered his way through the crowd and plucked at Chirpy Cricket's sleeve.

"Don't you think--" he asked earnestly--"don't you think I ought to carry one of the banners myself?"

"Perhaps so!" answered Chirpy Cricket. He was so taken aback that he really didn't know what else to say. "Which one do you prefer?"

"I'd have to see them before I made a choice," Freddie Firefly told him in a more hopeful tone.

So Chirpy ordered Kiddie Katydid and Moses and Mehitable to produce their banners, which they had left leaning against the wall.

They brought them forth fearfully, each hoping that his--or hers--wasn't going to be taken away and handed over to Freddie Firefly to carry in the procession.

"Here are the banners!" Chirpy Cricket said to Freddie. "Which one do you like best?"

Freddie looked at the banners and read them slowly, for he was not a good reader.

The first that he examined was the one Moses Mosquito had brought. And this is what it said:

WHY FUSS ABOUT A BITE, IF IT MAKES SOMEBODY ELSE HAPPY?

"I don't care for that one at all," Freddie Firefly announced. And he turned then to Kiddie Katydid's banner, which he spelled out with a good deal of trouble, because it was not so well printed.

This banner made the following announcement:

HONEST TO GOODNESS, I DIDN'T DO IT!

"Why, I don't know what that's all about!" Freddie exclaimed impatiently. "Let me see the third one!" So he looked next at the banner of Mehitable Moth, which seemed to please him better, as he read it aloud:

DON'T WORRY, MRS. GREEN! I'LL CALL AT THE FARMHOUSE BEFORE FALL.

"That's better!" cried Freddie Firefly. "I'll carry this banner with a great deal of pleasure. And I can call at the farmhouse to-night--if Farmer Green's family doesn't go to bed too early."

But there was one difficulty about Freddie's plan. Mehitable Moth did not like to have her banner, which she had made with great pains, taken away from her like that. And she drew Chirpy Cricket to one side and began talking to him in an undertone.

Soon he turned again to Freddie Firefly, saying, "She thinks that if you're going to carry her banner in the procession you ought to let her take your light."

"Oh, I can't do that!" Freddie exclaimed quickly. "I wouldn't THINK of doing that!"

"It would be only fair, it seems to me," Chirpy Cricket observed.

"Well, I won't do it, anyhow," Freddie declared. "I'd stay out of the procession first. And so would all my relations, too."

Chirpy Cricket began to look worried. And it was no wonder. For he knew he could have no torchlight procession without the Firefly family. But pretty soon he cheered up noticeably.

"I know what you can do!" he announced. "You can ride on top of Mehitable Moth's banner and keep flashing your light on it!"

VII
THE TORCHLIGHT PARADE

At last the torchlight procession was about to begin its march. Chirpy Cricket took his place at its head, as leader. And close behind him came Mehitable Moth, gaily bearing her banner aloft, with Freddie Firefly perched on top of it, and flashing his greenish-white light so that its rays fell full upon the words, which told Farmer Green's wife not to worry, because Mehitable Moth agreed to pay her a call before cold weather set in.

It would be hard to say which was the prouder--the person under the banner or the one on top of it. Anyhow, Chirpy Cricket was prouder than both of them together, because his torchlight procession promised to be a great success.

"Are you ready?" he cried, looking back at the marchers, who stretched behind him in a long line beside the stone wall.

Everybody shouted "Aye, aye, sir!" So Chirpy Cricket pranced away across the meadow, wearing a broad smile. Probably he had never before looked quite so cheerful.

But he had not gone far before something happened that drove the smile from his face, replacing it with a dark frown. He had glanced behind him, because he wanted--quite naturally--to look at that long line of lights twinkling through the night. And to his distress he saw that Freddie Firefly's relations were flying helter-skelter in all directions. They had bolted out of the line and were dancing off across the meadow after a fashion that no torchlight procession ought to follow.

"Stop! Stop!" Chirpy Cricket called.

Even as he spoke, as many as a dozen lights flashed past him and went flittering on across the fields.

Really, the only ones besides Chirpy that had stayed in the line as they should were Mehitable Moth, who still carried her banner right behind him, and Freddie Firefly, who sat on top of the banner.

And even Freddie Firefly was becoming restless. When he saw his brothers and cousins go dancing off in the dark he couldn't help wanting to dance too.

"You'd better hurry!" he said to Chirpy Cricket. "Those fellows--" he pointed to the dozen that had just passed them--"those fellows have got ahead of you. And it looks to me very much as if you were out of line."

Chirpy Cricket stared at Freddie Firefly in astonishment.

"Do you think so?" he exclaimed. "I don't see how it happened."

"Neither do I!" Freddie Firefly said. "But if I'm to stay in the procession I certainly can't sit on this banner any longer. And besides, if I'm going to call on Farmer Green's wife I shall have to travel faster than we're moving now."

Since they were then standing stock-still in the meadow, there was a good deal of truth in what Freddie Firefly said.

"But you don't need to call on Mrs. Green!" Chirpy Cricket cried. "That's not your banner, you know. It belongs to Mehitable Moth."

"I'm afraid Mrs. Green has heard I'm coming; and I don't want to disappoint her," Freddie replied.

And then he sprang from his perch and went zigzagging away.

One might think that Chirpy Cricket would have been quite upset by the breaking up of his torchlight procession. But being naturally cheerful, he merely smiled and said that it was plain that the Fireflies were a very flighty family.

VIII
BUSTER'S SCHEME

About the time summer was half gone, Buster Bumblebee's mother, the Queen, began to worry. She was afraid her workers were not going to make enough honey for her family's needs.

Then came a few days of steady rain, when the workers of the Bumblebee family couldn't venture away from home, on account of getting their wings wet. And of course the Queen was terribly upset.

"I don't know what to do!" she kept exclaiming. "The days are already growing shorter. It's a pity the honeymakers can't work in the dark."

Buster Bumblebee happened to hear his mother talking in that fashion with some of the older members of the family. And he spoke up at once and said:

"I know of a plan that might help."

Nobody paid the slightest attention to his remark, because the whole family thought that Buster was not only fat and lazy, but somewhat stupid as well.

"I know of something you could do that would help," he persisted, in a much louder voice. "The honey-makers could work after dark if you'd only get the Firefly family to furnish lights for them."

A number of Buster's relations snickered when they heard his plan. It struck them as being too silly for anything. But his mother, the Queen, looked very thoughtful.

"I'm not sure but that this boy has a good idea," she observed, much to the surprise of the others. "For a long time I've been waiting for him to say something worth listening to. And now I do believe he has had a happy thought at last." She turned to Buster. "How did you chance upon this scheme?" she asked him.

"Oh, the notion just came to me. I didn't have to WORK, to think of it," Buster explained. And he wondered why everybody laughed.

You know, Buster Bumblebee was so lazy that he never would lift a finger to do a stroke of work. And now the word "work" had a very funny sound, coming from his mouth.

"How could we get the Firefly family to help us? Have you thought of a way to do that?" Buster's mother said to her son.

"N-no, I haven't," he admitted. "But I'd go straight to Freddie Firefly and tell him what's wanted."

"Suppose you do that, then," said the Queen.

"You wouldn't call that WORKING, would you?" Buster inquired anxiously. Having long since promised himself that he would never work, of course he didn't want to break his word.

His relations--that is, except his mother--couldn't help tittering when Buster said that. But to tell the truth, they were beginning to be the least bit jealous of Buster Bumblebee and his plan. When the Queen frowned at them severely, each of them tried to look as if it had been somebody else that laughed.

Then the Queen assured Buster that paying a call on a person couldn't be said to be work.

"You go and talk with Freddie Firefly," she directed him, "and if your plan proves to be a success, it will then be your turn to laugh at others."

IX
FREDDIE'S PROMISE

Buster Bumblebee did not find Freddie Firefly very easily. It was a sunny afternoon; and if Freddie was flashing his bright light, Buster was unable to see it. But at last he spied Freddie eating a meal of pollen in the meadow. "How would you like to work for my mother, the Queen?" Buster asked him.

"I don't believe I'd care to, thank you," Freddie Firefly answered, with a mouth so full of food that Buster heard him only with great difficulty.

"I'll wait a moment, until you have finished your lunch," said Buster.

"You'd better not!" Freddie Firefly told him. "It will be dark by that time. And Chirpy Cricket tells me your family always goes to bed at sunset."

"So we do!" Buster agreed. "But my mother, the Queen, is going to order her honey-makers to work overtime for the present. And she wants you and your family to furnish lights so they can see what they're doing." "Oh! That's different!" Freddie Firefly exclaimed. "I thought she wanted me to help make honey. And that's something I know nothing about. ... But when it comes to furnishing a light, I'm certainly a shining success." Freddie then laughed heartily. And much to his surprise, Buster Bumblebee gave him several hard slaps on the back, which hurt him not a little.

"Don't do that!" Freddie Firefly cried.

"I thought you were choking," Buster, explained.

Freddie Firefly shook his head.

"I was joking," he said.

"Well, I didn't make much of a mistake; for joking and choking sound about the same," Buster Bumblebee replied.

"I hope your mother's honey-makers can tell the difference," Freddie Firefly grumbled. "If they can't, I certainly don't care to spend a night in their company."

"Oh, you won't have any trouble with them. They'll be working so busily that they'll hardly notice you," Buster Bumblebee assured him.

So Freddie Firefly promised to be at the house of the Bumblebee family, in the meadow, at dusk. And he said he would try to bring plenty of his relations with him, so that there might be one of them to light the way for each of the honey-makers.

And then Buster Bumblebee hurried away to tell his mother the news.

The Queen praised Buster for what he had done, telling him that in her opinion he would soon be the wisest person in Pleasant Valley--not even excepting old Mr. Crow and Solomon Owl.

Buster was so pleased that he made up his mind to stay awake that evening, in order to see the workers start out for the clover field after dark with Freddie Firefly and his relations. But when sunset came, Buster simply couldn't keep from falling asleep.

Not until the next morning did he know how his plan had turned out. And since it proved to be less successful than he had expected, perhaps it was just as well that he was not present to hear the remarks that were made about him.

Even Freddie Firefly said things about Buster that night that would not have been at all pleasant to listen to.

X
DRAWING LOTS

Buster Bumblebee's mother told her forty-nine honey-makers that Freddie Firefly and at least forty-eight of his relations were expected at the Bumblebees' house at dusk.

"Each of the Fireflies will furnish each of you with a light," the Queen explained, "so you'll be able to go to the clover field almost as easily as you do in the daytime. You're to work until midnight. And after that you may sleep until the trumpeter wakes you at dawn."

The Queen's announcement did not please the honey-makers in the least. They were an ill-tempered lot, anyhow. And when things did not go to suit them they sometimes made themselves most disagreeable.

Of course they didn't dare grumble in the Queen's hearing. But behind her back they spoke their minds quite freely.

"It's all the fault of that boy Buster," they told one another. "If he hadn't suggested his horrid plan to his mother we wouldn't have to work half the night and lose half our sleep."

"I wish he was here now!" one of the honey-makers exclaimed fiercely. "I'd make it hot for him!"

Usually the honey-makers began to grow very drowsy at that time of day (it was then late in the afternoon). But now they were so angry that they were not the least bit sleepy. Their own buzzing kept them awake. And the Queen was glad that it was so, because she herself never could have stopped so many of them from going to sleep. And even then, if the truth must be known, the Queen wished that she might go to bed. Never in all her life had she been up so late before.

"I wish the Fireflies would hurry!" she exclaimed as she stood at the front-door of her house and looked across the fast darkening field.

As she watched anxiously, the Queen soon spied a light, which kept growing brighter and brighter, until at last Freddie Firefly dropped down before her. He took off his cap and made a low bow.

"Here I am, Queen!" he said.

"Where's the rest of your family?" Buster Bumblebee's mother asked him.

"They all had to go to a dance down by the swamp," Freddie Firefly explained. "They wanted me to go with them; but I had promised your son that I'd be here at dusk. And of course I wouldn't think of breaking my promise."

Well, the Queen was terribly disappointed.

"You never can furnish enough light for my forty-nine workers!" she cried.

"Perhaps not!" Freddie admitted. "But I'd be glad to take one of them to the clover-patch to-night, just as a trial, you know."

The Queen said that that was a good idea. And the honey-makers, who had come outside the house, all agreed that it was a fine suggestion. But not one of them wanted to go with Freddie.

"Then you'll have to draw lots," the Queen told them severely.

When the honey-makers heard that, one of them tried to slip away. But the Queen saw her and called her back.

Then they drew lots. And strange to say, the worker who had tried to escape proved to be the unlucky one who was doomed to go to the clover field with Freddie Firefly and gather clover nectar until midnight.

Unluckily for Freddie, she was the worst-tempered person in the whole Bumblebee household. And when she saw that she alone of the whole family was going to lose half her night's sleep you may be sure she felt very surly.

Freddie noticed a wicked gleam in her eyes. And he began to wish he had gone to the dance over near the swamp.

XI
PEPPERY POLLY

Freddie Firefly felt quite uncomfortable as he started off toward the clover field, together with the angry honey-maker. It had not made him feel any more at ease when the Queen of the Bumblebees told him the worker's name. It was Peppery Polly.

"Don't go too fast!" Peppery Polly told Freddie Firefly. "And I'll tell you now that I'll make it warm for you if you try to play any tricks on me to-night."

As a matter of fact, Freddie hadn't thought of such a thing as playing a single trick on her. But Peppery Polly's warning at once put that very idea into his head. So he began to try to think of a good joke that would bother her. And before they had crossed the meadow Freddie Firefly turned to Peppery Polly Bumblebee and said:

"That light off there must be in the farmhouse."

Now, never having been out at night before, his companion wanted to see all the strange sights. So she stopped at once and looked around.

"How bright the light is!" she said. "Are you sure the farmhouse isn't on fire?"

Not receiving any answer, she turned her head. And to her dismay, she couldn't see Freddie Firefly anywhere.

"Oh! Oh! Where are you?" she cried. She was terribly frightened to be left alone in the dark. "Come back--please come back!" she begged.

"Why, here I am!" said Freddie Firefly.

And wheeling about quickly, Peppery Polly found him clinging to a blade of grass right behind her.

Freddie had been hiding under a plantain leaf, so that she couldn't see his light. But Peppery Polly didn't know what had happened.

"Did your light go out?" she inquired anxiously.

"If it did, I never noticed it," he replied.

"Well, don't you dare to leave me alone, no matter what happens!" Peppery Polly Bumblebee cried. "If you did, I'd never be able to find my way home in the dark."

"Don't worry!" Freddie said. "You're perfectly safe with me. ... What I'm wondering is whether I'm perfectly safe with you."

"You are--so long as you behave yourself," she declared. "But remember! I'll make it hot for you if you try any tricks on me! Don't forget that I carry a sting! And what's more, I know how to use it."

Her threat, however, failed to frighten Freddie Firefly. As soon as he saw that his companion was afraid of the dark, he ceased to be afraid of her. So he flashed his light impudently in her eyes.

"Come on!" he urged her with a grin which she could not see. "Let's get to the clover field, for I like to see people work."

"You do, eh? "snapped Peppery Polly.

"Yes! Watching others work is play for me," he remarked cheerfully. "And I hope to have as much fun to-night as I would have had if I'd gone to the dance over near the swamp."

"Are you fond of music?" Peppery Polly asked him suddenly.

"Am I?" he exclaimed. "I should say I was!"

"Then tell me how you like this," she said. And she began to sing the most terrible song that Freddie Firefly had ever heard in all his life.

XII
A TERRIBLE SONG

It was no wonder that Freddie Firefly grew uneasy again as he listened to the song of Peppery Polly Bumblebee, while they flew towards the clover field through the darkness. The chorus, especially, filled him with alarm. And he shuddered as the disagreeable honey-maker sang it:

"I've never learned to take a joke;   So if you try to trick me,   My sting in you I'll quickly poke--   You'll find that it will prick ye!   It feels like fire--though twice as hot.   And I would rather sting than not!"

"How do you like that?" Peppery Polly inquired, after she had finished her song.

"You have a beautiful voice," Freddie Firefly hastened to tell her.

"Yes--of course!" she agreed. "But I refer to the words. What do you think of them?"

"I think they're awful!" Freddie Firefly cried; for his companion had scared the truth out of him before he stopped to think how it would sound.

"Quite right!" said Peppery Polly. "I made up that song. And I flatter myself it's about the worst I ever heard." To Freddie Firefly's relief, she seemed quite pleased.

He was able to draw a deep breath again as they reached the field of red clover, where Peppery Polly Bumblebee settled quickly upon a clover-top and began sucking up the sweet nectar with her long tongue. For some time she worked busily without saying a word. And indeed, how could she have spoken with her tongue buried deep in the heart of a clover blossom?

But when she withdrew her tongue and flitted from one clover-top to another, she never failed to fix her wicked eyes on Freddie Firefly and demand "more light--and be quick about it!"

Since no harm had yet fallen him, he began to wonder after a while if Peppery Polly's bark was not worse than her bite--or perhaps it would be better to say that he wondered if her song was not worse than her sting. Anyhow, he knew that he was very tired of her masterful way of speaking to him. And he soon determined to play another trick on her.

"Here's a big blossom you haven't tasted!" he called to her suddenly. And Peppery Polly--thinking that Freddie meant a clover blossom-- hastened to a bloom that Freddie pointed out to her.

She settled upon it quickly. And the next moment Peppery Polly gave a sharp cry of mingled rage and pain.

"What's the matter?" Freddie Firefly asked her.

"Matter!" she exclaimed. "It's a thistle--and I've pricked myself badly."

"Why, so it is a thistle blossom!" said Freddie Firefly. "It's about the same color as a clover head; and I suppose you didn't know the difference in the dark."

"The question is, did YOU know the difference?" Peppery Polly screamed-- for she was terribly angry.

"Really, I must decline to answer when you speak to me in such a tone," said Freddie Firefly. And he was quite surprised that the furious honey- maker didn't dart towards him and try to sink her sting into him.

But nothing of the sort happened. And Freddie soon saw that Peppery Polly was in some kind of trouble.

XIII
CAUGHT BY A THISTLE

Y ou'll have to help me," Peppery Polly Bumblebee said to Freddie Firefly through the darkness. "If you'd been a little less stingy with that light of yours I wouldn't have made the mistake of thinking this thistle was a clover blossom."

"Well, there's nectar in it, isn't there?" he inquired.

"I suppose so," she answered. "But I can't get it. And I'm so daubed with the sticky stuff that's spread right where I put my feet that I can't free myself."

Freddie flew quite close to her and flashed his light upon her. And he saw that she had spoken truly.

"What a pity!" he exclaimed.

"Don't stop to talk!" the honey-maker snapped. "Just help me to get away from this thistle. And THEN you can talk all you want to. In fact, I'll give you something to talk about."

Freddie Firefly was not so dull-witted but that he knew she intended to punish him for sending her to the thistle blossom.

"I'll go back to your house and bring somebody to help you, if I can," he said. "Don't you see that it wouldn't be safe for me to try to pull you loose? I might get stuck there myself. And we'd be prisoners for the rest of the night."

Peppery Polly hadn't thought of that. And she was inclined to believe that there might be some such danger.

"You may go for help," she said at last. "But please remember that there's no time to lose. The Queen won't like it at all when she hears about this accident, for she expected me to fetch home a good deal of nectar before midnight."

"I'll hurry. And I'll be back as soon as I can bring one of your fellow- workers with me," Freddie Firefly promised.

Since he was a person of his word, he went straight back to the home of the Bumblebee family in the meadow. Being used to finding his way about after dark, Freddie had no trouble reaching the Bumblebees' home. But rousing the household was an entirely different matter. Though he pounded his hardest at their door, none of the Bumblebee family heard him. Having always slept from sunset till dawn without once waking, they were wrapped in such heavy slumber that not one of them knew what was going on.

To be sure, the family trumpeter--who awakened the household each morning and was a somewhat lighter sleeper than the others--the trumpeter claimed after-ward that she DREAMED that she heard somebody at the door that night. But that was all the good that came of Freddie Firefly's efforts.

After trying his best to rouse Peppery Polly's people, Freddie Firefly at last grew discouraged. He saw that the Bumblebee family was bound to sleep until dawn came, no matter what happened.

He reflected, then, that there were two things he could do. He could go back alone to the clover field and try to set that ill-tempered worker free--and no doubt get stung by her for his pains. Or he could go to the dance of the Fireflies over near the swamp, and have a delightful time.

"Let me see!" Freddie mused aloud. "I promised Peppery Polly that I'd come back with one of her own people--IF *I* COULD. And since I can't do that, I ought not to go back to the clover-patch at all. For if I did, it would be about the same as breaking a promise. ... No! I'll go to the dance instead!" And away he flew.

Luckily the dance was not half finished when he reached it. And he had such a pleasant time that he forgot all about that Bumblebee worker, stuck fast to the thistle blossom.

But you may be sure that Peppery Polly did not forget him. After her friends set her free the following morning she spent the whole day looking for Freddie Firefly.

But he lay very low. And all the rest of the summer he shunned the clover field--and the flower garden, too.

XIV
JENNIE JUNEBUG

On the day--or rather, on the night--when he first met Jennie Junebug, Freddie Firefly was ill at ease. In fact it might be truthfully said that he was quite upset.

One beautiful, warm, dark night early in the summer Freddie was hurrying to join a big family party which was already gathering in the hollow beyond the hill.

He was scooting along through the damp air, flashing his light at the rate of about thirty-six times a minute, when a heavy body bumped into him and knocked him head over heels upon the grass-carpeted ground.

It was no wonder that he felt upset. And he felt quite peevish, too, as he picked himself up and looked about him to see what had happened.

The next moment he was flashing his light into the blinking eyes of an enormous fat person, who seemed to be dazed, either by the shock of the collision or by the light--Freddie Firefly couldn't tell which.

"Why don't you look where you're going?" Freddie cried impatiently. "You knocked the breath out of me. And you almost broke one of my legs." The next instant he was heartily ashamed of himself; for he saw, to his surprise, that he was talking to a lady. "Oh! I beg your pardon!" he cried. "Ex--excuse me! I hope you're not seriously injured?"

"Oh, no!" wheezed the fat lady. "I'm all right. It's no matter, I assure you. I'm quite used to running into things after dark."

Freddie Firefly didn't quite like being referred to as a THING. But he was too polite to say so.

"You ought to be careful," he told the strange fat lady. "It's dangerous for one of your weight--"

"Oh, don't!" she exclaimed quickly. "PLEASE don't tell me I'm fat! I've tried every remedy I know and I can't lose a single pound!"

"Don't you think that flying makes you thinner?" Freddie Firefly asked her.

But the stout person shook her head dolefully.

"It only seems to make me bigger," she groaned.

"Then why do you do it?"

"Oh, I just adore flying!" she cried. "Don't you?"

Freddie Firefly admitted that he did like to fly. And he was sorry, the next moment, that he had made such a statement. For the fat lady blinked happily at him. And clasping her hands together, she said:

"Oh, do let's fly together, then!"

Freddie Firefly was so taken aback that at first he couldn't think what to say. But at last he managed to stammer a reply.

"Why--why--I--I'll be glad to, but I don't even know your name!" he told her.

"It's Jennie Junebug," she explained, as she fanned herself with a fan made from a white clover leaf.

"You're a newcomer in these parts, aren't you?" Freddie Firefly inquired.

"I just arrived here this month," she informed him. "This is the month of June, you know. And I'm one of the well-known Junebug family. ... I already know who you are," she continued. "You've been pointed out to me. You are Freddie Firefly; and you can't deny it."

XV
THE FAT LADY'S SECRET

Somehow, the longer Freddie Firefly talked with Jennie Junebug, the more he wished that he might fly off and leave her there in the meadow. But he had just the same as told her that he would be glad to fly with her. And he really didn't see how he could escape that unpleasant duty.

"Well, we may as well move on," he said at last. "Where were you going when we ran into each other?"

"Oh, nowhere in particular!" she answered. "Where were YOU going?"

Freddie Firefly had to bite his lip to keep from telling her that he had been on his way to a family party in the hollow beyond the hill. He certainly didn't want to go there in the company of that strange fat lady.

"I WAS going over the hill," he faltered at last. "But I'd rather stay here in the meadow with you."

"How nice of you to say that!" Jennie Junebug murmured. "And now let's begin flying at once!" she said.

So they rose into the air. But they hadn't flown more than a few feet when Jennie once more banged squarely into her companion.

It was a terrific blow. And Freddie Firefly soon found himself lying flat on the ground. He was so nearly stunned that he scarcely knew what had happened.

"What fun!" the fat lady gurgled right in his ear, with a horrible laugh. "Come! Let's do it again!"

"Do it again!" Freddie Firefly repeated after her, as a sudden fear gripped him. "Do you mean to tell me that you ran into me ON PURPOSE?" "Why, certainly!" she replied. "Running into a light is more than half the fun of flying."

Her terrible secret was out at last. If Freddie Firefly had been older and wiser he would have known, in the beginning, that his first collision with the fat lady was no accident. The whole Junebug family were alike in one respect: preferring to fly at night, whenever they saw a light anywhere they made straight for it as fast as they could fly. Sometimes they landed with a crash against one of the farmhouse windows. Sometimes they struck the lantern, if Farmer Green happened to be car-rying it across the farmyard. It really made little difference to a Junebug what he-- or she--hit, so long as it gleamed brightly out of the night.

Well, Freddie Firefly saw at last that he was in a terrible fix. He knew now why Jennie Junebug had asked him to fly with her. It was on account of his flashing light! And the dreadful creature actually expected him to fly for her so that she might have the pleasure of bowling him over every time he rose into the air.

Such a practice was disagreeable, to say the least. Indeed, Freddie Firefly thought it was positively dangerous, for him.

"Come! Come!" Jennie Junebug urged him playfully, even while he lay on the ground trying to get his breath. "If you don't hurry and fly some more I shall knock you over right where you are!"

Freddie Firefly answered her with a faint moan. He couldn't run away from her. So he thought of hiding. But he had promised to fly with her. And she was a lady.

What could he do?

XVI
FREDDIE'S ESCAPE

There was really nothing Freddie Firefly could do except struggle to his feet and try to think at the same time. Flashing his light upon Jennie Junebug he saw that she was looking at him fondly. And that made him detest her more than ever.

"You seem to be enjoying yourself," he said spitefully.

"Yes, indeed!" the fat lady exclaimed. "I haven't had such sport for a whole week. One of your cousins flew with me one night. And we had a fine time. No doubt we'd be enjoying each other's company yet, if I hadn't had a bit of bad luck."

"What was that?" Freddie Firefly asked her quickly. He thought that if he could only keep his dreadful companion TALKING, perhaps she would forget about FLYING--and knocking him down. "What was your bad luck?" he repeated impatiently.

Jennie Junebug paused and wiped her eyes.

"It was dreadful!" she said at last, as soon as she could control her shaking voice. "It was the worst accident that ever happened to me. ... Your cousin broke his neck!"

Although Freddie Firefly sank back with a groan, she did not seem to notice him.

"Your cousin--" she continued--"your cousin was the easiest thing to knock down that I ever saw. Why, once I knocked him over thirty-three times in one minute--or in other words, as fast as he flashed his light. . . . I had struck him so many times that he was growing weaker. Earlier in the evening, when he flashed thirty-six times to the minute, he was a little too quick for me."

"Don't stop! Tell me more!" Freddie Firefly begged her, as the fat lady ceased talking and fanned herself rapidly. And then, while she continued to tell him about his unfortunate cousin, Freddie set his wits to work upon a plan to escape from the dreadful creature. He hardly knew what she was saying. But every time she paused he urged her on again with a "Yes, yes!" or a "Go on! Go on!"

At first a wild hope came to him that he might be able to keep her talking all night. Then, of course, he would be safe; because when daylight came she would no longer be able to see his light.

But he soon had to give up that plan, for he saw plainly enough that the fat lady was growing restless. And at last she told him flatly that she had talked all she cared to.

"I'm ready to fly now," she announced with an awful eagerness.

"One moment!" he said hastily. "Your fan--I see you've torn it! And if you'll let me take it I'll try to find you another just like it."

"Will you?" Jennie Junebug asked him gratefully. "And will you promise to come back just as soon as you've found me a PERFECT match for my fan?"

"I promise!" said Freddie Firefly, snatching the fan out of her hands in his haste. "Wait right here!" he cautioned her. And then he leaped into the air and started away.

BANG! He hadn't flown longer than forty-six seconds when Jennie Junebug floored him again.

"I simply couldn't resist hitting you once more!" she said sweetly. "And now, hurry! Or I shall never be able to let you leave me."

Freddie Firefly needed no more urging. Though he was sore in every limb (and he had a great many!) he made his escape quickly.

All the rest of the night he worked hard, trying to find a white clover leaf that exactly matched the one that Jennie Junebug had carried for a fan. But every single clover leaf was different from Jennie's in one way or another. Freddie Firefly had hoped that it would be so. For if he had found one precisely like Jennie Junebug's, he would have had to take it to her, as he had promised.

How long the fat lady waited for him in the meadow, Freddie Firefly never knew. And to tell the truth, he didn't care. He was too happy because he had escaped the fate of his cousin, to bother his head over Jennie Junebug.

XVII
BAD BENJAMIN BAT

For a long time Benjamin Bat had had his eye on Freddie Firefly. And every time the two met, Benjamin stopped to tell Freddie how plump he was growing.

"You're just about ready to--AHEM!" Benjamin remarked when he came upon Freddie in Farmer Green's dooryard one fine evening.

"What did you say?" Freddie inquired.

"Never mind!" Benjamin Bat answered. "I was only talking to myself. It's a habit I have."

"You're a queer one!" Freddie Firefly exclaimed. "But it's no wonder. People say that you've hung upside down so much that the inside of your head is all topsy-turvy."

"When he heard that remark Benjamin Bat promptly flew into a rage.

"You'd better be careful!" he warned Freddie. "I don't allow anybody to talk to me like that."

"Oh! You mustn't mind what I just said," Freddie Firefly replied. "I was only talking to myself--AHEM AHEM!"

But strange to say, Freddie's answer failed to please Benjamin.

"Your remark was very disagreeable, anyhow," he declared.

"Well--so was yours," Freddie retorted stoutly.

"How can you say that?" Benjamin Bat inquired with a sly look. "I didn't finish it, did I?"

"No!" replied Freddie. "But you can't fool me. I know what you meant, as well as you do."

And straightway Benjamin Bat looked most uncomfortable, because he had been thinking that Freddie Firefly HAD BECOME PLUMP ENOUGH TO EAT.

Indeed, there was only one thing that kept Benjamin from devouring Freddie Firefly right then and there. And that was Freddie's flashing light. Yes! Benjamin Bat was afraid that if he touched Freddie Firefly he would get burned.

Once a forest fire broke out while Benjamin was asleep in the woods. And he didn't wake up until the tree in which he was hanging by his heels had begun to blaze. Luckily he escaped with his life. But the flames singed the tips of his wings and gave him such a fright that ever afterward he feared a fire or a light of any kind. And now he did wish that Freddie Firefly would put out his light, just for a short time. So he said, after a few moments:

"Don't you think you ought to stop flashing your light?"

"Do you mean--" asked Freddie--"do you mean that I ought to keep it glaring steadily all the time?"

"Oh, no!" Benjamin Bat replied hurriedly. "I mean that you ought to put it out for a while."

"Why should I do that?" Freddie Firefly wanted to know.

"To please Farmer Green, of course," Benjamin replied glibly. "Don't you know that a light always draws mosquitoes? And it can't be very pleasant for Farmer Green to have half the mosquitoes in the neighborhood crowding into his dooryard."

"What would be the use of my putting out my light, when all my relations are flashing theirs?" Freddie asked.

"Well, maybe they'd follow your example," Benjamin Bat suggested. "And just think what a good turn you'd be doing Farmer Green!"

XVIII
PLEASING FARMER GREEN

Now, when Benjamin Bat spoke of his doing Farmer Green a good turn, Freddie Firefly looked puzzled.

"What has Farmer Green ever done for me?" he inquired.

"What has he done?" Benjamin cried. "Hasn't he furnished you a fine meadow in which to dance at night? And doesn't he let you come here in his door-yard whenever you please? I should think THAT was something to be thankful for!"

"Now that you speak of it, I don't know but that you're right," Freddie Firefly admitted, "though I never thought of such a thing before." And not wishing to be ungrateful to Farmer Green, he promptly put out his light.

Of course, that was just what Benjamin was waiting for. And since he could see perfectly in the dark, without a moment's warning he rushed straight at Freddie Firefly, with his mouth wide open.

If Freddie hadn't happened to flash his light just at that moment he would never have flashed it again.

As soon as Benjamin Bat saw the greenish-white gleam he was so afraid of getting burned--not knowing that Freddie's light could not harm him--he was so afraid that he swerved sharply to one side and zigzagged about the yard for a few seconds.

But he soon returned to speak to Freddie Firefly once more.

"You made a good beginning," he told Freddie. "But you turned your light on again too quickly. Just keep dark until I tell you to shine, and with a little practice you'll be able to do the trick very well. And Farmer Green will certainly be pleased. Now, just try it again!"

But Freddie Firefly could not forget how terrible Benjamin had looked a few moments before. And he began to suspect that Benjamin Bat was playing a trick of his own.

"It seems to me," said Freddie, "that you are a little too anxious about Farmer Green."

"Oh! no, indeed!" Benjamin Bat declared. "Farmer Green is a fine man. He's a great friend of mine. He furnishes me a whole tree near the swamp, in which I sleep every day. If you passed that way any time between dawn and sunset you could see me hanging by my heels from one of the branches."

"Just where is your tree?" Freddie Firefly inquired.

Having no idea that Freddie could do him the slightest harm, Benjamin Bat explained that his special, favorite tree was a great cedar, which stood close to the old bridge that crossed Black Creek, at the lower end of the swamp.

"I know where that is; and I'll go over there to-morrow and take a look at you," Freddie Firefly remarked.

"Do!" said Benjamin Bat.

"And I'll bring Solomon Owl with me," Freddie added. "For I know he'd like to see you, too."

"Don't!" cried Benjamin Bat. "Oh, don't do that!"

"What's the matter?" Freddie Firefly asked Benjamin Bat. "Why don't you want me to fetch Solomon Owl to your tree, to see you hanging by your heels when you're fast asleep?"

"Solomon Owl is no friend of mine," Benjamin Bat explained with a shudder. "He'd eat me in a minute, if he could catch me."

XIX
BENJAMIN FEELS GUILTY

Freddie Firefly and Benjamin Bat faced each other in Farmer Green's dark dooryard.

"Yes!" Benjamin Bat's thin voice quavered. "Don't EVER bring Solomon Owl to my tree in the daytime. Although he doesn't see so well when it's light as he does at night, he could catch me without much trouble when I was asleep. And he would eat me in a minute--or only half a minute, maybe."

"Well, wouldn't you like that?" Freddie Firefly inquired, as if he were greatly surprised.

"Certainly not!" said Benjamin Bat. "You talk like a--AHEM!"

"Perhaps I do," Freddie Firefly retorted. "But I should think it would be just as jolly for you to be eaten by Solomon Owl as it would be for me to be eaten by you."

Benjamin started violently.

"What in the world ever put such a strange idea into your head?" Benjamin Bat cried. He was greatly astonished, for he had not supposed that Freddie Firefly suspected exactly what was in his mind.

"You put that idea into my head yourself," Freddie Firefly said very sternly.

And the moment Benjamin Bat heard that, he felt very sheepish. But unlike most people who feel ashamed, he did not hang his head. Strangely enough, Benjamin Bat was never so proud as when his head hung lower than his heels. And he had a habit, when he felt guilty or uncomfortable, of RAISING his head, instead of dropping it. So now he lifted his head very high.

And by that tell-tale sign Freddie Firefly knew at once that Benjamin Bat would have flushed with dismay, had he only known how.

"You're a rascal!" Freddie cried fiercely, flashing his light again and again in Benjamin Bat's eyes, until that gentleman blinked so fast that it seemed as if his eyes must be in danger of turning inside out.

"You'd better be off!" Freddie Firefly shouted. "And if you ever come to me again, coaxing me to put out my light--so you can eat me--I'll certainly bring Solomon Owl to your tree when you're asleep there."

Still Benjamin Bat made no move. Yet he wanted to go away because he was in terror of being burned by Freddie Firefly's light. But he did not dare turn his back upon Freddie Firefly and his light and fly away. And he began to be sorry that he had never learned to fly backwards.

"Please--" Benjamin Bat stammered at last--"please do me a favor. I'm not feeling very well. I'm afraid I'm going to be ill. Maybe you'll be good enough to go and ask my friend Farmer Green to step outside his house a moment. Just tell him I'm in trouble," he whined.

"Trouble!" Freddie Firefly sneered, for he knew well enough--by this time--that Benjamin Bat was scared, though he couldn't quite guess the reason for Benjamin's fright. "You'll be in worse trouble if I show Solomon Owl where you sleep in the daytime."

"Stand back!" Benjamin Bat shrieked suddenly. "You'll singe my wings if you're not careful!"

Then Freddie Firefly knew exactly what Benjamin feared. And he was so amused that he couldn't help taking a turn around the dooryard, to dance and laugh and shout.

And when he came back to the place where he had left Benjamin Bat, that odd gentleman had vanished.

The terrified Benjamin had floundered away toward the swamp. And never, afterward, did he have a word to say to Freddie Firefly.

But whenever Freddie Firefly caught sight of Benjamin Bat's dark shape, flitting in a zigzag path across the moon, he always cried out in a loud voice:

"Look out, Benjamin Bat! Mr. Moon will singe your wings if you're not careful."

XX
MRS. LADYBUG'S ADVICE

Finding himself face to face with Mrs. Ladybug one night in Farmer Green's meadow, Freddie Firefly noticed, even before she spoke, that the little lady was not in a cheerful mood. In fact, she frowned at him darkly and pointed one of her knitting needles straight at him as she began to speak.

"You're terribly careless with that light of yours," she said. "People are always warning me that my house is on fire and telling me that I'd better hurry home. Now--" she added--"now I think I've discovered the reason why my friends are forever worrying about fire. No doubt when they give me such advice they have seen you prowling around my house with that light of yours; and they think that if you haven't already set my house on fire, you're just a-going to."

When Freddie Firefly saw that Mrs. Ladybug was making Benjamin Bat's mistake of thinking that his light could start a blaze, he had to smile.

"Nonsense!" he cried. "I'm always very careful, Mrs. Ladybug, when I'm near your house. You know that I wouldn't want your charming children to burn up."

And now Mrs. Ladybug pointed her other knitting needle at Freddie.

"Well, if you're not careless, you're silly, anyhow," she snapped. "I wouldn't object so much to your light if only you'd put it to some good use. But as long as I've known you--and that's several weeks--I've never seen you do anything but caper about the meadow and dance." And then Mrs. Ladybug began to knit furiously, as if to show Freddie Firefly that she was never idle, even if she did spend a good deal of time away from home. "Do you intend always to fritter your nights away as you do now?" she inquired.

"What else could I do? I should like to know--" Freddie began.

"Why not use your light in some kind of work?" Mrs. Ladybug asked him.

"What work, I should like to know--" Freddie said. And since Mrs. Ladybug did not at once answer him, he added: "I don't believe you can suggest anything--can you?"

"Oh, yes, I can!" she declared quickly. "I was thinking. That's why I didn't reply sooner. Probably you don't know that I have helped many youngsters to begin to work. For instance, it was I that told Daddy Longlegs to help Farmer Green with his harvesting." Little Mrs. Ladybug felt so proud of herself that she dropped a stitch without noticing it.

"Daddy Longlegs! HE'S not young!" Freddie Firefly exclaimed.

"Oh! yes, he is! He's not so old as you think," Mrs. Ladybug replied. "He's just about your age. And if he can work, you certainly can."

"But I didn't know that Daddy Longlegs was working for Farmer Green," Freddie Firefly said.

"He tried to, one day. But the wind blew too hard. ... It wasn't really Daddy's fault," Mrs. Ladybug explained. "And you ought not to attempt to work on windy nights, either," she went on. "For your light might go out, and then there'd be a terrible accident."

XXI
ALL ABOUT TRAINS

What do you mean?" Freddie Firefly asked little Mrs. Ladybug. "What accident could happen if the wind blew out my light?" And he laughed very hard, because he knew that no gale was strong enough even to dim his greenish-white gleams.

"Why," replied Mrs. Ladybug, "the train would strike you and be wrecked. You see," she continued, "I have everything planned for you. You're going to spend your nights on the railroad tracks, signalling the trains."

Well, Freddie Firefly rather liked Mrs. Ladybug's idea. And though he knew that she was mistaken about some things, he began to think that perhaps she was quite wise, after all.

"Aren't you afraid I might set fire to the trains?" he inquired slyly.

"No, indeed!" she answered. "You'd stop them, you know, before they ran over you."

"But I don't know how to make a train stop," he objected. "I've never worked on a railroad in all my life."

"Why, it's simple enough," said little Mrs. Ladybug. "When a train came along you would stand on the track right in front of it and wave your light." And while she smiled at Freddie Firefly as if to say, "You see how easy it is," she dropped six more stitches out of her knitting--and never found them, either.

Freddie Firefly, however, did not smile at all. On the contrary, he looked some-what worried.

"Are you sure it's safe?" he asked her. "If the train failed to stop, with me on the track in front of it--"

"Don't worry about that!" cried little Mrs. Ladybug. "You'll never amount to anything if you worry. And if you don't wish to fritter away your time dancing in this meadow, you'll take my advice and begin to work at once."

"I'll think about the matter," said Freddie Firefly. And then he added somewhat doubtfully: "It's a long way to the railroad."

"Pooh!" Mrs. Ladybug exclaimed. "Old Mr. Crow often visits it. And if he can fly that far, at his age, a youngster like you ought not to mind the trip."

"Perhaps you know best," Freddie Firefly told Mrs. Ladybug at last. "I'll take your advice just this once, and I'll see how I like the work. But there's another question I'd like to ask you: What will the trains do after they stop?"

While laughing over Freddie's question Mrs. Ladybug shook so hard that she unravelled sixteen rows of her knitting before she could stop.

"Bless you!" she cried, as soon as she could speak. "I don't know what the trains will do. That's their affair--not yours nor mine. Everybody's aware that trains are made for two purposes--to start and to stop. But I never should think of being so rude as to ask them WHY, or WHAT, or WHEN, or WHERE."

So Freddie Firefly thanked Mrs. Ladybug most politely. He was sure, now, that she was one of the wisest persons in the whole valley. No doubt, he thought, she knew almost as much as old Mr. Crow, or even Solomon Owl. And he wished he knew half what she did.

"I'll start for the railroad track at once," Freddie told Mrs. Ladybug. And waving his cap at her, while she waved her knitting at him, he set forth towards the village, the lights of which twinkled dimly in the distance.

XXII
WORK ON THE RAILROAD

Freddie Firefly did not intend to go into the village itself. He expected to travel only as far as the railroad tracks, where they curved around a bend in the river before stretching straight away towards the town.

Though he spent a much longer time in making the journey than old Mr. Crow ever took, Freddie at last reached the railroad, where he promptly sat himself down between the rails to wait for a train. And there Freddie Firefly stayed all alone, in the dark, with nothing to keep from feeling forlorn except the croaking of a band of noisy frogs in a pool near-by.

After a while Freddie began to grow so weary of his new task that he wished he had never taken Mrs. Ladybug's advice.

"I don't believe I like working," he said with a sigh, as he thought of the good time his family was having at that very moment, dancing in Farmer Green's meadow.

And then all at once he heard a faint whistle, far off down the valley. And a little later a low rumble caught his ear--a rumble which grew louder and louder until at last it turned into a roar, just as a stream of light shot around the curve in the track ahead of him, which followed the bend of the river.

Freddie Firefly was startled. He couldn't think what made that long lane of light. And he was about to jump into the bushes and hide when he saw all at once that it was exactly what he had been waiting for.

"It's a train!" he cried aloud. And he began flashing his light bravely while he swayed from side to side, for Mrs. Ladybug had told him that he must swing his light--if he expected to stop the train.

And all the while the train tore on towards Freddie Firefly. To his great surprise it showed not the slightest sign of stopping. And in spite of what Mrs. Ladybug had said, Freddie Firefly began to be afraid that it wasn't going to pause at all.

He soon saw that if he did not do something quickly the train would run over him. But by the time he had made up his mind to jump off the track, out of harm's way, it was too late for him to escape in that fashion.

So Freddie Firefly crawled hurriedly into a chink beneath the railroad tie on which he had been sitting. And with a horrible scream the train thundered over him. To Freddie's dismay it paid no heed to his flashing light, though he thought it must surely have seen that signal.

Those were terrible moments for Freddie Firefly, while the train was passing above him. The frightful noise, the trembling of the ground, the rush of the air--all those things made him wonder whether he could ever reach home again, alive and unharmed. He was even more scared than he had been when he found himself in the power of that dreadful creature, Jennie Junebug.

XXIII
WHY FREDDIE WAS GLAD

Even after the train had rushed shrieking into the village two miles away, and the echoes had grown still, Freddie Firefly cowered in his hiding-place on the railroad track, crouched in the chink beneath one of the ties.

At last he crept out, trembling in every limb. But in spite of his terror he skipped off the track very spryly.

Safe at one side of the rails, which gleamed in the moonlight, Freddie felt himself all over, to make sure that he had broken no bones.

"I seem to be unhurt," he mused. "But never, never again will I listen to anything that Mrs. Ladybug says."

And having made himself that solemn promise, he hurried away toward Farmer Green's meadow, which he reached just before dawn.

As he crossed the fields he thought that he smelled smoke. But he couldn't see a blaze anywhere. And when he came to the meadow he was so eager to dance that he forgot to ask anybody if there had been a fire.

Luckily he arrived in time to take part in the last dance of the night. And after the dance was over he astonished all his family with the strange tale that he told them.

Before going to their homes all Freddie's relations gathered around him to listen to his story of the night's adventure. And there were many "Ohs" and "Ahs" when he reached the point where the train ran over him.

"You're lucky you didn't have a leg cut off," his favorite cousin remarked, "though that wouldn't have been so bad as losing a wing."

Freddie Firefly shuddered.

"Anyway, you're better off than Mrs. Ladybug is," somebody piped up.

"Why, what's happened to her?" Freddie Firefly inquired.

"Haven't you heard?" several of his cousins cried.

"No! no!" he shouted.

"Her house caught fire to-night, while she was away from home," they explained.

"I thought I smelled smoke as I was coming back from the railroad," Freddie observed. And then a sad picture came into his mind.

"And Mrs. Lady bug's children--" he began breathlessly.

"Oh! The neighbors saved them," his favorite cousin said. "They're only slightly scorched. But their ma's house is ruined."

Then, to everybody's great surprise, Freddie Firefly began to dance up and down and sing with joy.

"Oh, I'm so glad! Oh, I'm so glad!" he chanted over and over again.

His relations could scarcely believe that he was quite himself.

"His fright on the railroad must have injured his mind," they said to one another. "Or perhaps the train ran over his head when he didn't know it." They could think of no other reason for Freddie's queer actions. Always before he had seemed too kind-hearted to rejoice over another person's ill luck.

"What do you mean?" three hundred voices shouted. "Why are you glad?"

"I'm glad I tried to stop the train," Freddie Firefly answered, "because now Mrs. Ladybug can't say that I set her house on fire. She knows that I was working on the railroad to-night. And nobody can be in two places at the same time."

The Codes Of Hammurabi And Moses
W. W. Davies

QTY

The discovery of the Hammurabi Code is one of the greatest achievements of archaeology, and is of paramount interest, not only to the student of the Bible, but also to all those interested in ancient history...

Religion   **ISBN:** *1-59462-338-4*   **Pages:132**

MSRP $12.95

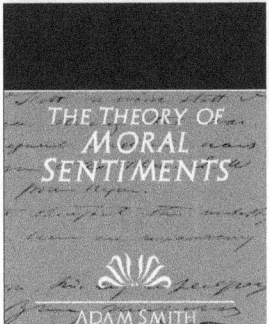

The Theory of Moral Sentiments
Adam Smith

QTY

This work from 1749. contains original theories of conscience amd moral judgment and it is the foundation for systemof morals.

Philosophy   **ISBN:** *1-59462-777-0*   **Pages:536**

MSRP $19.95

Jessica's First Prayer
Hesba Stretton

QTY

In a screened and secluded corner of one of the many railway-bridges which span the streets of London there could be seen a few years ago, from five o'clock every morning until half past eight, a tidily set-out coffee-stall, consisting of a trestle and board, upon which stood two large tin cans, with a small fire of charcoal burning under each so as to keep the coffee boiling during the early hours of the morning when the work-people were thronging into the city on their way to their daily toil...

Pages:84

Childrens   **ISBN:** *1-59462-373-2*   *MSRP $9.95*

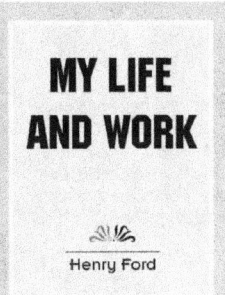

My Life and Work
Henry Ford

QTY

Henry Ford revolutionized the world with his implementation of mass production for the Model T automobile. Gain valuable business insight into his life and work with his own auto-biography... "We have only started on our development of our country we have not as yet, with all our talk of wonderful progress, done more than scratch the surface. The progress has been wonderful enough but..."

Pages:300

Biographies/   **ISBN:** *1-59462-198-5*   *MSRP $21.95*

The Art of Cross-Examination
Francis Wellman

I presume it is the experience of every author, after his first book is published upon an important subject, to be almost overwhelmed with a wealth of ideas and illustrations which could readily have been included in his book, and which to his own mind, at least, seem to make a second edition inevitable. Such certainly was the case with me; and when the first edition had reached its sixth impression in five months, I rejoiced to learn that it seemed to my publishers that the book had met with a sufficiently favorable reception to justify a second and considerably enlarged edition. ..

QTY

Pages:412

Reference   ISBN: *1-59462-647-2*   *MSRP $19.95*

On the Duty of Civil Disobedience
Henry David Thoreau

Thoreau wrote his famous essay, On the Duty of Civil Disobedience, as a protest against an unjust but popular war and the immoral but popular institution of slave-owning. He did more than write—he declined to pay his taxes, and was hauled off to gaol in consequence. Who can say how much this refusal of his hastened the end of the war and of slavery ?

Law   ISBN: *1-59462-747-9*   **Pages:48**

MSRP $7.45

QTY

Dream Psychology Psychoanalysis for Beginners
Sigmund Freud

Sigmund Freud, born Sigismund Schlomo Freud (May 6, 1856 - September 23, 1939), was a Jewish-Austrian neurologist and psychiatrist who co-founded the psychoanalytic school of psychology. Freud is best known for his theories of the unconscious mind, especially involving the mechanism of repression; his redefinition of sexual desire as mobile and directed towards a wide variety of objects; and his therapeutic techniques, especially his understanding of transference in the therapeutic relationship and the presumed value of dreams as sources of insight into unconscious desires.

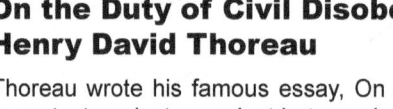

Psychology   ISBN: *1-59462-905-6*

Pages:196

MSRP $15.45

QTY

The Miracle of Right Thought
Orison Swett Marden

Believe with all of your heart that you will do what you were made to do. When the mind has once formed the habit of holding cheerful, happy, prosperous pictures, it will not be easy to form the opposite habit. It does not matter how improbable or how far away this realization may see, or how dark the prospects may be, if we visualize them as best we can, as vividly as possible, hold tenaciously to them and vigorously struggle to attain them, they will gradually become actualized, realized in the life. But a desire, a longing without endeavor, a yearning abandoned or held indifferently will vanish without realization.

Pages:360

Self Help   ISBN: *1-59462-644-8*   *MSRP $25.45*

QTY

QTY

The Rosicrucian Cosmo-Conception Mystic Christianity by *Max Heindel*   ISBN: *1-59462-188-8*   **$38.95**
The Rosicrucian Cosmo-conception is not dogmatic, neither does it appeal to any other authority than the reason of the student. It is: not controversial, but is: sent forth in the, hope that it may help to clear...   New Age/Religion Pages 646

Abandonment To Divine Providence by *Jean-Pierre de Caussade*   ISBN: *1-59462-228-0*   **$25.95**
"The Rev. Jean Pierre de Caussade was one of the most remarkable spiritual writers of the Society of Jesus in France in the 18th Century. His death took place at Toulouse in 1751. His works have gone through many editions and have been republished...   Inspirational/Religion Pages 400

Mental Chemistry by *Charles Haanel*   ISBN: *1-59462-192-6*   **$23.95**
Mental Chemistry allows the change of material conditions by combining and appropriately utilizing the power of the mind. Much like applied chemistry creates something new and unique out of careful combinations of chemicals the mastery of mental chemistry...   New Age Pages 354

The Letters of Robert Browning and Elizabeth Barret Barrett 1845-1846 vol II   ISBN: *1-59462-193-4*   **$35.95**
by *Robert Browning* and *Elizabeth Barrett*   Biographies Pages 596

Gleanings In Genesis (volume I) by *Arthur W. Pink*   ISBN: *1-59462-130-6*   **$27.45**
Appropriately has Genesis been termed "the seed plot of the Bible" for in it we have, in germ form, almost all of the great doctrines which are afterwards fully developed in the books of Scripture which follow...   Religion/Inspirational Pages 420

The Master Key by *L. W. de Laurence*   ISBN: *1-59462-001-6*   **$30.95**
In no branch of human knowledge has there been a more lively increase of the spirit of research during the past few years than in the study of Psychology, Concentration and Mental Discipline. The requests for authentic lessons in Thought Control, Mental Discipline and...   New Age/Business Pages 422

The Lesser Key Of Solomon Goetia by *L. W. de Laurence*   ISBN: *1-59462-092-X*   **$9.95**
This translation of the first book of the "Lernegton" which is now for the first time made accessible to students of Talismanic Magic was done, after careful collation and edition, from numerous Ancient Manuscripts in Hebrew, Latin, and French...   New Age/Occult Pages 92

Rubaiyat Of Omar Khayyam by *Edward Fitzgerald*   ISBN:*1-59462-332-5*   **$13.95**
Edward Fitzgerald, whom the world has already learned, in spite of his own efforts to remain within the shadow of anonymity, to look upon as one of the rarest poets of the century, was born at Bredfield, in Suffolk, on the 31st of March, 1809. He was the third son of John Purcell...   Music Pages 172

Ancient Law by *Henry Maine*   ISBN: *1-59462-128-4*   **$29.95**
The chief object of the following pages is to indicate some of the earliest ideas of mankind, as they are reflected in Ancient Law, and to point out the relation of those ideas to modern thought.   Religion/History Pages 452

Far-Away Stories by *William J. Locke*   ISBN: *1-59462-129-2*   **$19.45**
"Good wine needs no bush, but a collection of mixed vintages does. And this book is just such a collection. Some of the stories I do not want to remain buried for ever in the museum files of dead magazine-numbers an author's not unpardonable vanity..."   Fiction Pages 272

Life of David Crockett by *David Crockett*   ISBN: *1-59462-250-7*   **$27.45**
"Colonel David Crockett was one of the most remarkable men of the times in which he lived. Born in humble life, but gifted with a strong will, an indomitable courage, and unremitting perseverance...   Biographies/New Age Pages 424

Lip-Reading by *Edward Nitchie*   ISBN: *1-59462-206-X*   **$25.95**
Edward B. Nitchie, founder of the New York School for the Hard of Hearing, now the Nitchie School of Lip-Reading, Inc, wrote "LIP-READING Principles and Practice". The development and perfecting of this meritorious work on lip-reading was an undertaking...   How-to Pages 400

A Handbook of Suggestive Therapeutics, Applied Hypnotism, Psychic Science   ISBN: *1-59462-214-0*   **$24.95**
by *Henry Munro*   Health/New Age/Health/Self-help Pages 376

A Doll's House: and Two Other Plays by *Henrik Ibsen*   ISBN: *1-59462-112-8*   **$19.95**
Henrik Ibsen created this classic when in revolutionary 1848 Rome. Introducing some striking concepts in playwriting for the realist genre, this play has been studied the world over.   Fiction/Classics/Plays 308

The Light of Asia by *sir Edwin Arnold*   ISBN: *1-59462-204-3*   **$13.95**
In this poetic masterpiece, Edwin Arnold describes the life and teachings of Buddha. The man who was to become known as Buddha to the world was born as Prince Gautama of India but he rejected the worldly riches and abandoned the reigns of power when...   Religion/History/Biographies Pages 170

The Complete Works of Guy de Maupassant by *Guy de Maupassant*   ISBN: *1-59462-157-8*   **$16.95**
"For days and days, nights and nights, I had dreamed of that first kiss which was to consecrate our engagement, and I knew not on what spot I should put my lips..."   Fiction/Classics Pages 240

The Art of Cross-Examination by *Francis L. Wellman*   ISBN: *1-59462-309-0*   **$26.95**
Written by a renowned trial lawyer, Wellman imparts his experience and uses case studies to explain how to use psychology to extract desired information through questioning.   How-to/Science/Reference Pages 408

Answered or Unanswered? by *Louisa Vaughan*   ISBN: *1-59462-248-5*   **$10.95**
Miracles of Faith in China   Religion Pages 112

The Edinburgh Lectures on Mental Science (1909) by *Thomas*   ISBN: *1-59462-008-3*   **$11.95**
This book contains the substance of a course of lectures recently given by the writer in the Queen Street Hail, Edinburgh. Its purpose is to indicate the Natural Principles governing the relation between Mental Action and Material Conditions...   New Age/Psychology Pages 148

Ayesha by *H. Rider Haggard*   ISBN: *1-59462-301-5*   **$24.95**
Verily and indeed it is the unexpected that happens! Probably if there was one person upon the earth from whom the Editor of this, and of a certain previous history, did not expect to hear again...   Classics Pages 380

Ayala's Angel by *Anthony Trollope*   ISBN: *1-59462-352-X*   **$29.95**
The two girls were both pretty, but Lucy who was twenty-one who supposed to be simple and comparatively unattractive, whereas Ayala was credited, as her Bombwhat romantic name might show, with poetic charm and a taste for romance. Ayala when her father died was nineteen...   Fiction Pages 484

The American Commonwealth by *James Bryce*   ISBN: *1-59462-286-8*   **$34.45**
An interpretation of American democratic political theory. It examines political mechanics and society from the perspective of Scotsman James Bryce   Politics Pages 572

Stories of the Pilgrims by *Margaret P. Pumphrey*   ISBN: *1-59462-116-0*   **$17.95**
This book explores pilgrims religious oppression in England as well as their escape to Holland and eventual crossing to America on the Mayflower, and their early days in New England...   History Pages 268

www.bookjungle.com *email: sales@bookjungle.com fax: 630-214-0564 mail: Book Jungle PO Box 2226 Champaign, IL 61825*

QTY

The Fasting Cure *by Sinclair Upton* ISBN: *1-59462-222-1* **$13.95**
In the Cosmopolitan Magazine for May, 1910, and in the Contemporary Review (London) for April, 1910, I published an article dealing with my experiences in fasting. I have written a great many magazine articles, but never one which attracted so much attention... New Age/Self Help/Health Pages 164

Hebrew Astrology *by Sepharial* ISBN: *1-59462-308-2* **$13.45**
In these days of advanced thinking it is a matter of common observation that we have left many of the old landmarks behind and that we are now pressing forward to greater heights and to a wider horizon than that which represented the mind-content of our progenitors... Astrology Pages 144

Thought Vibration or The Law of Attraction in the Thought World ISBN: *1-59462-127-6* **$12.95**
by William Walker Atkinson Psychology/Religion Pages 144

Optimism *by Helen Keller* ISBN: *1-59462-108-X* **$15.95**
Helen Keller was blind, deaf, and mute since 19 months old, yet famously learned how to overcome these handicaps, communicate with the world, and spread her lectures promoting optimism. An inspiring read for everyone... Biographies/Inspirational Pages 84

Sara Crewe *by Frances Burnett* ISBN: *1-59462-360-0* **$9.45**
In the first place, Miss Minchin lived in London. Her home was a large, dull, tall one, in a large, dull square, where all the houses were alike, and all the sparrows were alike, and where all the door-knockers made the same heavy sound... Childrens/Classic Pages 88

The Autobiography of Benjamin Franklin *by Benjamin Franklin* ISBN: *1-59462-135-7* **$24.95**
The Autobiography of Benjamin Franklin has probably been more extensively read than any other American historical work, and no other book of its kind has had such ups and downs of fortune. Franklin lived for many years in England, where he was agent... Biographies/History Pages 332

Name	
Email	
Telephone	
Address	
City, State ZIP	

☐ **Credit Card**   ☐ **Check / Money Order**

Credit Card Number	
Expiration Date	
Signature	

Please Mail to: Book Jungle
PO Box 2226
Champaign, IL 61825
or Fax to: 630-214-0564

ORDERING INFORMATION

web: *www.bookjungle.com*
email: *sales@bookjungle.com*
fax: *630-214-0564*
mail: *Book Jungle PO Box 2226 Champaign, IL 61825*
or PayPal *to sales@bookjungle.com*

Please contact us for bulk discounts

DIRECT-ORDER TERMS

**20% Discount if You Order
Two or More Books**
Free Domestic Shipping!
Accepted: Master Card, Visa,
Discover, American Express

www.ingramcontent.com/pod-product-compliance
Lightning Source LLC
Chambersburg PA
CBHW081306200626
46813CB00018B/3283